THE BOY WHO OWNED THE FOREST

stories by
Elizabeth J.M. Walker

Illustrations by Nicholas Beckett

Handersen Publishing, LLC
Lincoln, Nebraska

The Boy Who Owned the Forest
Handersen Publishing, LLC
Lincoln, Nebraska USA

Text copyright © 2019 Elizabeth J.M. Walker
Illustrations copyright © 2019 Nicholas Beckett
Cover copyright © 2019 Handersen Publishing, LLC
Cover Design by Nicholas Beckett
Interior Design by Nichole Hansen

Summary: A collection of seven stories that will whisk you away to fantastical places. Learn to follow your own passion, deal with grief and depression, face your fears, and develop strength through adversity.

Library of Congress Control Number: 2018910942
Handersen Publishing, LLC, Lincoln, Nebraska

Paperback ISBN: 978-1-947854-36-9
Hardback ISBN: 978-1-947854-37-6
eBook ISBN: 978-1-947854-38-3

Publisher Website: www.handersenpublishing.com
Publisher Email: editors@handersenpublishing.com

For James and Lillian
~E.J.M.W.

For my mother, Helen
~N.B.

Lauren,
Hope you enjoy
the stories.
Elin J.M.Walsh

Contents

There once was a boy who owned a forest. One could even say he was the king of this forest, although no official title was actually given. He was simply the boy who owned the forest.

This forest stretched from one horizon to the next, full of plum-colored trees that bore silver fruits the size of chubby pigeons. When the fruits would get too heavy for their tree's branches, they would fall to the ground and burst into silver dust that would settle in a thick layer, so that the entire forest floor was covered in sparkling silver dust.

The forest was a quiet, serene place. For this reason many great scholars lived there, so they could study, invent, and create in peace. Each scholar had their own personal dwelling that they made with their own hands and means.

The inventor's home was a tall silver tower with many spinning things, and shiny things, and things that gave off smoke in different colors: blue, red, and dusty rose.

The composer's house was made of bricks and had a thatched roof. In it was a grand piano, a cello, a tambourine, and many other instruments with many other names.

The writer's house was a beautiful log cabin made with the plum-colored trees of the forest. Inside were shelves of books and a desk with pots of ink, quills, and parchments scattered everywhere.

The dancer's house was made of brick like the composer's, but the roof and one wall were completely made of glass, so that you could see into the house, and see that all of the other walls had mirrors on them. The dancer liked to see the beautiful nature that inspired him to dance, and he also liked to perform for the forest animals, who would watch intently through the glass. There were many other homes in the forest, but none quite as interesting as these four.

The boy's house was a hodgepodge of all of these. He asked the inventor to build his home tall like hers, and he asked the composer to thatch its roof, and he asked the writer to make parts of his home with interlocking logs, and he asked the dancer to make part of his ceiling out of glass so he could see the stars at night. The four gladly built the boy's odd home, for he had granted them all permission to dwell in his beautiful forest.

One day the boy decided to visit the scholars. First he went to the inventor's tower for breakfast. She greeted him kindly and used a system of pulleys and ropes to raise him up to the highest level of the tower, where they could see that the forest truly did reach as far as the eye could see. The inventor brewed tea in an odd-shaped pot that gave off bright blue steam, and served it to the boy with a stack of delicious pancakes.

After breakfast, she taught the boy how the pulleys worked, and all about her experiments and the different colored smoke. The boy was enthralled.

"What does this do?" he'd ask, and the inventor would tell him.

"How does this work?" he'd ask, and the inventor would explain.

The boy asked to borrow books from her, so he could read more about inventing. She happily let him borrow as many books as he could carry.

Next, the boy headed to the composer's house for lunch. The composer made tuna sandwiches with alfalfa sprouts. After they'd eaten, the composer sat at her grand piano and played a tune.

"That was beautiful!" the boy exclaimed. "I'd love to be able to play music."

The composer handed the boy a wooden flute and gave him a quick lesson. She told him what he should practice when he was at home, and the boy thanked her and promised that he would.

Next, the boy arrived at the writer's house for dinner. The writer made delicious meat and veggie pies with tasty gravy. As they ate, the writer told his latest story to the boy, who listened in rapture.

"That was magnificent!" the boy said. "I think I could make up a story."

The writer told him about plot and character traits. He gave him a quill and parchment, so the boy could work on his writing.

Next, the boy went to the dancer's home. He watched with the squirrels and rabbits through the glass as the dancer flew through the air and seemed to turn on the spot like a top. When the dancer finally stopped his performance, he smiled at the boy and beckoned him to come in for a nighttime snack of creamy yogurt with sweet fruit.

"How did you do that?" the boy asked. "When you jumped in the air and went–" The boy attempted to mimic the dancer's graceful leap.

"That's quite good," the dancer told him. "I could begin to train you, and one day you could dance upon a stage for an audience."

"Really?" the boy asked.

"Yes, I do think so," the dancer said. He showed the boy some simple steps, and corrected him when he made a misstep here and there. The dancer told him what to practice when he got home.

By the time the boy who owned the forest returned to his house he was tired. He took out the books the inventor had lent him, and then the wooden flute the composer had gifted him, and then the quill and parchment the writer had given him, and then he cleared the space so he could practice the dance steps the dancer had shown him.

"But what shall I do?" the boy mused aloud. "I don't have time for all of them at the moment, and I'm dreadfully tired. I suppose I should go to bed."

And so the boy changed into his pajamas and climbed under the covers.

The boy had so much fun with the four scholars that a few days later he went to visit them again. The inventor wanted to discuss the information that was in the books the boy had borrowed, but the boy hadn't read them.

"Tsk-Tsk!" said the inventor. "How do you expect to become an inventor like me if you don't read your books? And think about new ideas? And discuss them with other inventors?"

"I don't know," the boy answered sheepishly. "I'll read the books and come back."

Next, the boy went to the composer's for lunch.

"Come, I'll play the cello and you play your wooden flute and we can play this fun little duet I composed," the composer said eagerly. She handed the boy a sheet of music.

"But I...I haven't learned to read music yet," the boy told her.

"Well, I guess we can wait until you learn. Come back when you have, won't you?"

"Yes, I'll come back," the boy said, and headed off to the writer's for dinner.

"Oh, I'm so glad to see you," the writer said. "I've been writing a story about two young sisters and the ocean, but I've stumbled upon some dreadful writer's block. Why don't you read to me what you have written, to help inspire me?"

"I'm sorry, I haven't been able to write anything," the boy confessed to the writer.

"Oh well, perhaps you have writer's block too," the writer said with a chuckle. "But when you do write something, be sure to stop by and read it to me."

"Yes, as soon as I'm done writing a story I'll come read to you," the boy promised, and headed off to the dancer's house.

"I'm glad you've come," the dancer told him. "I've been eager to see how you've improved with the steps I showed you. If you've mastered them, I'd love to be able to teach you some more. Maybe we could even do a little duet."

"I...I'm not sure I remember the steps you showed me last time," the boy told the dancer.

"Haven't you been practicing them?" the dancer asked.

"No, I haven't. But if you show me again, I promise I will practice. And when I come back I'll be so good we can do a duet."

The dancer went over the first steps he'd taught the boy, and showed him some more steps to practice at home. The stars began to twinkle in the evening sky, so the boy decided to head home for the night.

The next day, the boy who owned the forest made sure to read up on inventions, learn to play the notes from the sheet music, attempt to write a story, and practice the steps the dancer had shown him. He had great fun doing so, even though he was so busy he forgot to eat.

The next day, he went to visit the four scholars, but none of them were quite satisfied, even though he had practiced.

"Why can't I be as good as you?" the boy asked all four of them. They all told him the same thing: he had to practice hard and devote all his time to his skill.

The next day, and the days that followed, he read and played and wrote and practiced so diligently that he forgot to sleep as well as eat. Yet, in all his anxiousness to be talented at so many skills and to impress his teachers, he did not notice the state of his forest.

The silver fruits were growing dull and were shriveling up. Instead of growing ripe and silver and then falling to the ground to cover the forest floor in silver dust, they were simply dying, so there was no more beautiful sparkling silver carpeting the forest floor. The plum-colored trees were beginning to lose their vibrant color. The scholars did notice, and it worried them—so much so, that it affected their studies and creativity. They all decided to give the boy who owned the forest a visit.

The four scholars were surprised to see one another at the boy's home and to learn that he had been visiting them all. The composer rang the doorbell, and the boy hesitated answering it—he was in the middle of writing an exciting story. But the doorbell rang again, and he removed himself from his story.

"Oh, what are you all doing here?" he asked when he opened the door. "Shall I prepare some food?"

"No, that won't be necessary," the inventor told him.

"Do come in," the boy said.

"Have you all come to talk to the boy about the forest?" the composer asked the others, and they all nodded.

"What about the forest?" the boy asked.

"Look," the dancer said, pointing out the window. "The forest is dying."

The boy looked out the window and gasped. "What's happened?"

"We don't know, we came to find out," the writer said.

"Perhaps it's because you've been spending too much time reading up on inventions," the inventor suggested.

"Reading up on inventions?" the composer questioned. "I thought perhaps it was because he was spending too much time learning to play the wooden flute."

"Inventions? Wooden flute?" the writer said. "I thought he had been working on a great work of literature!"

"And I thought he was practicing his dancing!" the dancer said.

"Have you been doing all these things?" the inventor asked. The boy nodded, his eyes cast to the floor.

"Perhaps that is why the forest is dying," the composer said.

"And perhaps that is why you can't write a great masterpiece. You aren't giving it your all," the writer said.

"And why you can't focus on your dancing," the dancer said.

"What should I do to save the forest?" the boy asked.

"I don't know. I don't have an invention that saves forests," the inventor told him sadly.

"It isn't our forest," the composer pointed out.

"No, I do not believe we can help you with this," said the writer.

"It's not our speciality," the dancer said.

"Our work," the inventor said.

"Our passion," the composer said.

"Our life's ambition," the writer said.

The boy sighed.

"We should leave now," said the inventor. The others agreed. They left the boy alone in his hodgepodge house of towers, logs, thatch, and glass.

The boy climbed up into his tower and looked out onto the horizon, and at his neglected forest that was now a dull shade of gray.

"What have I done?" he whispered. "All I wanted to do was invent, and play music, and write, and dance. All I wanted was to be talented, like all the others who live in my forest. I wish I had a special talent."

A wind blew, rustling the canopy of the forest, as if saying, "I am your forest. Take care of me."

The boy sighed. He'd known his whole life he owned the plum-colored forest that reached to all horizons, and bore silver fruits the size of chubby pigeons. He knew in his heart and he knew in his soul. He also now knew in those same places that trying to have another talent would be fruitless, and that his friends in the forest only had one great talent, which was their heart and their soul.

And the more he thought about it, the more color returned to the bark and leaves of the trees. The silver fruits began to grow once more. Soon they would be big enough to fall from the branches and burst on the floor, spreading sparkling silver dust.

The boy quickly rushed to his pantry and packed a basket full of scones, a big fruit salad, and brownies. He ran to each of the four scholars' houses to invite them to a picnic.

"We're all very proud of you," the inventor said, once they had all begun to eat.

"Yes, it's wonderful that you've found your passion," the composer told him.

"And now the forest and all that dwell here can prosper once more," said the writer.

"Including yourself," the dancer said with a smile.

Just then, a plump fruit fell off the branch of a nearby tree and burst into silver dust when it hit the ground, sprinkling the inventor, the composer, the writer, the dancer, and the boy who owned the forest.

My mother died.

My mother used to play the piano.

My mother died, but Father kept the piano.

I would sometimes catch Father staring at the piano. It was as if he was willing it to play like Mother used to do every night after dinner while he did the washing up. He'd say, "It's a pleasure to do the dirty work when accompanied by such beautiful music." Then he'd fill up the sink with soapy water, Mother would play, and I would dance some childish made-up dance, which would make them both laugh.

I remember one night when Father was staring at the piano. The sink was piled high with dirty dishes. We were out of clean bowls and running low on spoons. I walked up to him and tapped him on the shoulder. He slowly turned to look at me. He had crying eyes, the kind that are red and sad.

"I could dance for you," I whispered. It was so quiet in the house, I felt it might fall apart if I made more noise than a whisper.

He shook his head and turned away from me, back to staring at the piano. I tiptoed back to my bedroom. I got out my crayons and drew a picture. The picture was of my mother, playing the piano. I hid it under my mattress, so Father wouldn't find it and be more sad.

Father wasn't the only one who missed Mother. I did too, and so did the piano.

One night I lay in bed, surrounded by darkness and silence. My night light had burnt out. I didn't want to ask Father to put a new light bulb in it—Mother used to do that for me. But I couldn't sleep in the dark. I lay awake. I heard a train go by in the distance: Choo-choo-chooooooooooo. I heard something moving down the hall. I thought maybe it was Father.

I went out into the hall, but Father wasn't there. At the end of the hall, the piano could be seen sitting in the living room, facing me. Its ivory keys looked like teeth. The sloping, ornate wood that sheet music and music books full of notes would rest against looked like a moustache.

The piano began to move.

I gasped and jumped back into my room. I heard it moving down the hall, toward the door to the outside. I peeked around the corner and saw the piano amble out the door. I could hear Father snoring. I crept out after the piano.

I had never been out in the night by myself. The moon was bright above and surrounded by stars, but it was still very dark. I saw the piano making its way down the street. A group of fireflies came down to fly around me. They guided my way through the ocean of darkness that lay between the islands of light from the street lamps.

The piano made its way to the little river that flowed by our neighborhood. The piano got into the river. With its feet on the bottom, the water was just deep enough to lap at its keys. The piano swam about in the water, and the current would push the keys down, making noise. But I wasn't entirely sure if the river knew what music was—it didn't sound like anything my mother used to play.

The wind came and sent a single shiver down my entire body.

"Piano, come back now!" I called to it. "I'm cold!"

The piano hesitated, and then followed me back to the house. I snuck back into my bed. Father was still snoring.

Maybe, I thought, as I drifted off to sleep, what the river needs is some music notes to read.

The very next night, I heard the train whistle in the dark. I slipped out of bed and into the hall just in time to see the piano go out the door. I grabbed some sheet music from Mother's box next to where the piano usually was, and began to follow it down the road. This night was darker than the one before, with thick, gray clouds in the sky. Low rumblings could be heard amongst the stars. A pitter-patter of rain began to fall.

The piano went to the river again, and the sky rumbled more, shaking the stars. Flashes of light could be seen in the distance as the stars fell from their spots in the sky. The rain began to fall harder.

"Piano come back!" I called as it slid down the muddy bank into the water. "It's going to storm, come back!"

But the piano wouldn't listen to me and the storm was now upon us. The wind ripped through the branches of the trees that lined the river.

I tried to get closer to the river, to give it the sheet music. I began to climb down the bank, but it was very muddy and I went sliding down into the water. I landed with a crash upon the piano's keys—a loud sound other than thunder filled the air. I placed the soggy sheet music on the piano.

"Play river, play!" I said, but the river didn't know how to play, even when it did have notes to read. The water was rising quickly, the river getting deeper from the rain. The current was pounding me against the piano.

"Come, piano, the river can't play you like Mother," I told it, trying to pull it out of the dangerous water. But the piano refused to move.

"I'll get lessons!" I told the piano. "I'll ask Father to send me to a piano teacher! I'll get lessons and learn how to play you, just like Mother!"

The piano shifted in the muddy river bottom, then pulled itself out of the river, with me clinging to it. We lay on the river bank, black leeches sticking to my legs, arms, and toes.

~

The next day after dinner, Father was staring at the piano once more. I tapped him on the shoulder.

"What is it, Chloe?" he asked without turning.

"Can I take piano lessons?" I asked him.

"No," he said.

"Why not?"

"I said no."

"But Mother said when I was old enough, she'd teach me to play."

"Mother isn't here to teach you."

"But she would have liked me to learn from someone else then," I said. "Wouldn't she?"

Father said, "No."

"But—"

"Go to bed."

It was much too early for bedtime, but I went anyway. I lay awake for a very long time, until it got dark, and then the train whistled. I knew the piano would be leaving the house and I wanted to follow.

It was raining again—pouring. The sky thundered and shot bright bolts of lightning down to earth. The piano escaped from the house, made its way down the street, and tumbled into the river. The piano let the current push it around. There were moments when I couldn't even see the piano in the crazy, deepening water.

"Piano! No!" I shouted, and jumped into the rushing water. The river nearly pulled me away from the piano, but I grabbed on.

"Piano, don't do this! Don't leave like Mother!" I said, but it didn't listen. It let itself be pulled along by the current, tumbling about through the muddy water, and I had to hang on with all my strength.

"I can't play you, piano!" I screamed through the storm. "Father won't let me! I can't play you piano!" I beat fiercely on the keys until my hands hurt. The notes were barely audible against the rush of the river and the roar of the storm.

"Don't leave like Mother, please!" I told it, now crying. "I'll learn to play, I'll learn somehow! I'll teach myself. I can't lose you, piano, you're all I have."

The piano pulled us out of the river. I lay on the bank next to it, gasping for air.

The next night was calm. The train whistled, and the piano made its way to the river, with me walking close behind. The piano sank into the still waters, and I followed. The piano waited patiently as I gently put my fingers on the keys, and I began to teach myself to play.

It took years, but every night we'd go down to the river and play together. I grew older, but my playing got better. Father never knew. He'd still stare at the piano, as all his hair turned gray. I wondered if I should play for him. I wondered if I was as good as Mother. Would my playing make him happy? Or would it make him sad?

I grew older still, and so did Father. His hair began to fall out. The piano and I continued our secret lessons in the river. Father never heard me play. But I wanted my own life. I wanted to move out on my own, but I knew Father wouldn't let me take the piano. I wasn't sure how I could continue without it. I decided I would remain with Father, and with the piano.

Then Father got sick. He was old and dying, and only had a few breaths left to breathe, every one of them like a countdown to the end. It was best I stay with him.

One night after dinner, I washed the dishes and then gave Father his medicine. I was headed to my room when I saw the piano, and I knew I had to play.

I went to the piano. For the first time in my life I played the piano indoors. In our home. I played a song Mother used to play.

Father called down the hall, weakly: "Marianne?"

I rushed to his bedside.

"No," I told him, sitting next to his bed and taking his hands in mine. "It was me, Chloe."

But he had gone.

SMACK. Pitter–patter, drip–drop, drip...SMACK.

Cornelia opened her eyes and looked into the darkness that coated her bedroom. Fat raindrops splattered against her window: pitter–patter, pitter–patter, SMACK. Cornelia did not think the last sound was a raindrop. Drip–drop, drip–drop. The rain dripped over the edge of the roof. Pitter–patter, drip–drop. SMACK.

Raindrops do not go SMACK, Cornelia felt sure of this. She sat up and pushed the blankets off her legs. She slipped out of bed and walked across her room to the window. She felt around in the darkness for the curtain's cord, and then pulled. She could see her dark window glistening with raindrops, each filled with the light of streetlights from the next street over. She could see the outlines of the fruit trees in her backyard, swaying, heavy with tart pears and bug–eaten apples.

SMACK.

Cornelia jumped and gasped as something small and white smacked itself against the wet window, and then quickly disappeared. She searched the dim light of the backyard to find where it had gone.

SMACK.

Cornelia jumped again. Was it a bird? What was it doing?

I suggest you opens the window, Timothy said, as he crawled across the windowsill. He was a tiny black house spider with little white spots—the kind of spider that jumps if you put your finger near it.

"It's raining," Cornelia told her arachnid friend.

It wants to comes in, insisted Timothy in his quiet little spider voice.

Cornelia swallowed nervously as she undid the window releases as quietly as possible, not wanting to wake her parents sleeping in the next room.

SMACK.

Cornelia had to quickly clamp her hand over her mouth to keep her scream from coming out, as the white thing hit the window again, directly in front of her face. She glared down at Timothy, who was descending on a fine thread of web from the windowsill. He stopped a few centimeters down, and swayed a little on his thread.

I thinks it's okay. It won't hurt you, he said.

Cornelia had no real reason to doubt the spider. She had been friends with him for quite some time, and he always seemed to have an innate knowledge about peculiar things—he was a talking spider, after all.

Cornelia slid the window open, and then pushed back the screen that was saturated with water. A cool wind blew through her soft, butter-colored hair, and a few drops of rain drifted in. Then something soggy and white flew by, brushing past her cheek before it began to haphazardly fly about her room. She slid the screen and window closed to stop the rain coming in, and then turned her full attention to whatever it was that she had just let inside.

She could hear a wet flapping noise moving around the room. Cornelia clicked on her faery-shaped night light, which filled the room with a bluish glow.

The thing flew by Cornelia's face, and she caught a better view of its papery nature—it appeared to be a flying booklet! It flew by once more, and this time she reached out and plucked it from the air. It fluttered in her hands and she cooooed at it, and said things like **there, there** in a gentle voice to make it calm down. Once it stopped moving, Cornelia could see it was indeed a little booklet of white papers. She gingerly turned the soggy pages to find words and pictures inside.

"What is it?" she asked Timothy.

I do nots know, he replied.

From that night on, Cornelia kept coming across similar little booklets of paper. They weren't all white: some were made of colored paper, or had colored stamping on the front. Some were held together with staples, and some were sewn together with pretty strands of embroidery floss, or dental floss, or pieces of twine. She would find them under rocks, or in the branches of trees, on bus seats, or blowing in the wind. In them she'd find writing about love and pain and happiness, stories and comics and recipes and rants and information and poems and photographs and lists of favorite things:

1. canned pineapple
2. chopsticks
3. old book smell
4. the sound mud makes when you step in it,
    and then pull your foot out

The little paper booklets made her happy, but some made her sad. And some she would read out loud to Timothy, before her parents came home from work and made perogies for dinner. Some she'd read to the squirrels in the forest. But the squirrels were usually more interested in climbing the trees and jumping from one branch to another, and going chitter-chitter-chatter while Cornelia tried to read to them.

No one else seemed to notice these little paper booklets, and sometimes people would look extra hard at what she was holding while she was reading on the bus. It reminded her of when she wore her Halloween costume in June—she'd been a witch. But she didn't mind people looking at her funny, because she loved the little booklets (just like she'd loved her witch costume too, with the lace up boots and pointy hat).

If you love them so much, maybes you should try making one of your own, suggested Timothy one night.

Cornelia thought that the house spider might be onto something, so she got out some pens and some paper and scissors and glue, and a pile of her mom's fashion magazines she said Cornelia could have for craft projects. With the help of Timothy, she wrote some stories and some lists of her favorite places and animals and insects, and made some pretty collages too. She even included an illustration of Timothy, which the spider was very pleased about. Then it was ready to all be folded and bound together: she used red embroidery floss. She read her little creation to Timothy and made sure to show him each page as she did so, just like her kindergarten teacher used to do in class.

I likes it, he told her. **You shoulds let others see it too.**

That night, Cornelia opened up her window. It was a calm night with no rain and little wind. She held her little paper booklet in her hands and told it to fly. Hesitantly, it fluttered from her hands but stayed near, flying around her outstretched arms.

"Go," she told it softly. It flew off into the night, into the world where someone else would find it. And she hoped it would make them as happy as the little booklets had made her.

Lucy crossed over the railway tracks and walked along the paved path in the summer heat. The cornstalks in the field next to her were reaching to the blue sky way above her head. A rollerblader skated down the path ahead, and a bicyclist was about to pass on her left. The wind rustled the cornstalks.

"Lucy..." a voice called from the cornfield, as the bicyclist whizzed by.

She stopped and noticed a parting in the cornstalks—just wide enough for her to enter.

She looked back to the tracks: no one was there. She looked ahead—both the bicyclist and the rollerblader had gone around the bend in the path. Lucy took one slow step toward the corn.

The wind rustled the cornstalks once more, and this time Lucy heard the words, "Come in, Lucy."

Lucy took another hesitant step forward. "Who's there? How do you know my name?"

"Come, Lucy." The cornstalks parted a little bit further. Lucy stepped into the cornfield, her heart beating wildly. The cornstalks were at least a foot above her head. She began to walk: a clear and distinct pathway through the cornstalks had opened up before her. She walked until she came to a fork in the path. Which way to go? Left or right? She chose to go right. But the pathway with the walls of cornstalks just kept going and going.

"Where am I?" Lucy called.

"You're so small..."

Lucy shivered, and the cornstalks began to grow around her, taller and taller, closer and closer to the sky—the darkening sky. She turned to leave, hastily trying to backtrack her steps, but only came to a dead end: a wall of cornstalks. She tried to push through, but they wouldn't budge, not even enough for Lucy, who was very little.

"Go forward, not back."

"I want out!" Lucy called, her heart now beating even fiercer. "Let me out!"

"Find your own way."

Lucy felt her eyes swimming with tears, and she hugged herself. The air was getting cold. She let the tears silently roll down her cheeks. Every time a tear fell to the ground, a colorful eggshell would appear, but Lucy did not notice.

"I think I've been here before!" Lucy said when she came to yet another dead end. She was about to continue her search for a way out when she felt something crunch beneath her sneaker. She lifted her foot to see a piece of shattered, mauve eggshell.

"Oh, I hope I didn't kill the poor baby bird," she said, but there was no yolk, and it was just a fragment of a much bigger egg.

"Leave it be," came the voice. But Lucy picked it up and cradled it in her hand. The cornstalks grew even taller, nearly blocking out the setting sun.

She found a piece of a blue eggshell. Then she found a yellow piece, then orange, and then green. As Lucy picked up the pieces, she realized that each cracked edge could be put together with the last—like the pieces of a puzzle. The egg was getting so big she had to cradle it in her arms and let it lean against her chest. Every time she found a piece of the shell, the voice would protest and the cornstalks would grow taller, yet Lucy felt stronger with each piece she fit together, and her tears had subsided.

Finally, she found a pink piece of broken shell that completed the egg. As soon as she fit it in, the egg's puzzle-like pieces smoothed over in a wave of light to form one silver egg. And the cornstalks rose until it was dark, and the only light came from the egg itself: a dull silver glow.

The egg grew warm and began to shake in Lucy's arms. And the cornstalks grew even taller. The egg cracked open and a tiny yellow beak popped out and began to chirp. Then a white wing, and another, and a whole bird the size of Lucy's head came flying out. It was a sleek white bird with a slender neck, black beady eyes, and a long tail that split into a fork, like a lizard's tongue. The egg shell fell and turned back into tears that sank into the ground.

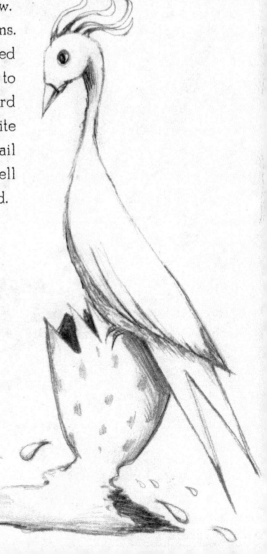

"Lucy, it is so dark!" the bird sang, and began to fly upwards, softly glowing silver-white. The bird broke through the cornstalk roof, and the pink light of the setting sun filtered in.

"I'll help you find the way out," the bird called. "Which way would you like to go?"

"Don't follow the bird."

"No, Lucy, let me help you. You don't belong here in this darkness," the bird explained, and flew down to perch on Lucy's shoulder. "Let me fly above, where I can see the maze of the cornstalk's twists and turns, and I will guide you out."

"Okay," said Lucy, thankful for her new bird friend.

"There are many exits though," the bird told her. "One leads to a castle where the bakers make lovely scones, another leads to a palace made of gold, another to my country where my kinfolk fly above great trees, another is a place that's very placid, and yet another is full of fire and excitement—"

"Please, I just want to go home to the paved path by the railroad tracks," Lucy told the bird.

The bird cocked her head to the side, and then flew up into the sky and disappeared from sight. She returned shortly, and landed once more on Lucy's shoulder. "I do not see this place you talk of, with paved paths and railways. You must choose another, and quickly! Soon the sun will be gone and we will be left in darkness."

"Let us go to your land then," Lucy said.

"Of course! You'll love it there!" the bird sang, and flew up into the sky, above the cornstalk maze. The bird guided Lucy, telling her which turns to take. Before she knew it, she was out of the growing darkness of the maze, and in a great green twilit forest where many birds of different colors, shapes, and sizes flew about.

"You are too big to sleep in my nest, but I'm sure my friend the great green bird won't mind if you sleep in her nest with her chicks," the white bird said, and told her which tree to climb.

Lucy climbed the tree and was greeted by a bird with sparkling emerald feathers. The bird was bigger than Lucy and had a giant nest where three smaller green birds nestled together. They welcomed her and let her snuggle in among their feathers. But even though the great green bird's nest was quite comfortable, Lucy could not sleep. One of the little green birds couldn't sleep either, and noticed Lucy's restlessness.

"What is wrong?" he chirped.

"I don't belong here," Lucy whispered back.

"True, you don't have wings. You'll never fit in here unless you have wings. I shall guide you to another world."

Lucy climbed down the tree, making sure to be quiet and not wake the others, while the young green bird flapped beside her. Once in the maze, Lucy noticed the cornstalks had returned to their original height—just above her head.

"I see a lovely castle. Humans live in castles, don't they?" the green bird called down to her.

"Yes, but I have never lived in a castle," Lucy said.

The cornstalks began to grow taller.

"Don't follow the bird."

"Oh, shush. I know the way," the green bird called. "Turn left here, little human."

The sun was beginning to rise just as they reached the gray, stone castle.

"I must leave you here. My mother will be worried about me," the green bird said, and flew off.

The castle looked large and daunting. Lucy thought about going back into the maze and finding her own way, but just then a plump maid came out of the castle and saw her.

"Why hello, young lady. Are you lost?"

"Well, I'm—"

"You look famished and tired! Come in, and I'll find you some food, then you can have a rest in a nice big bed. What do you say?"

Lucy was hungry, and very tired, so she agreed.

The maid gave her fresh baked scones with creamy butter, and a big dish of strawberries with real whipped cream, and even a plate of pancakes with syrup. When Lucy was stuffed, the maid led her up to a beautiful guest room with a four-poster bed. The sheets were made of silk, and lavender was sewn into the pillows to make them smell nice. Lucy was so exhausted she kicked off her sneakers and climbed into bed. She fell asleep as soon as she lay down.

When Lucy awoke after a good sleep, she wasn't quite sure where she was. She looked out the window and she could see the edge of the cornfield, and then she remembered. Her heart sank. The castle was lovely, but she still had to find her way home. It was twilight once more, and the sun was slowly sinking in a haze of orange and pinks. Lucy pulled on her sneakers and left the room.

She wandered down a corridor, and then a hall, and then down a spiral staircase, and then through another hall and down a staircase.

"Can I help you?" came a voice from behind her, as she walked down a corridor.

Lucy turned to see a young man in a blue velvet suit.

"I think I'm lost," Lucy told him.

"Where are you trying to go?"

"Out."

"Why?"

"I need to get to the cornfield, so I can find my way home."

"Really? Where are you from?"

"Somewhere else."

The young man was silent. "I'm sorry, I forgot to introduce myself. My name is Damien."

"I'm Lucy. Can you help me find my way out of the castle?"

"But it's getting dark. Why don't you stay here tonight?"

Just then, the plump maid came into the corridor.

"Oh, good evening, your majesty," she said, and curtsied to the young man.

"Good evening. Could you please find this young lady a room?" Damien asked her.

"But of course! I was just looking for her, so I could give her some supper. She arrived early this morning, and has been sleeping all day," the maid explained.

"May I join you for supper?" Damien asked Lucy.

"If you like, your maj—"

Damien shook his head and smiled. "Call me Damien, please."

"If you like," Lucy said nervously—she had never met royalty before.

A beautiful dinner was laid out for them with pineapples, and salads, and other colorful dishes featuring meats and sauces with fresh, green garnishes. Damien and Lucy talked and smiled and laughed all throughout dinner. They got along like old friends. Lucy completely forgot that he was a royal, and nearly forgot that she was lost.

"We're having a ball tomorrow evening. Will you stay for it?" Damien asked.

"I don't know...I really want to get home," Lucy told him.

"I would be very pleased if you could come to the ball. There's sure to be several dresses for you to choose from somewhere in the castle. And there'll be a great many interesting people and…"

"And…?"

Damien sighed. "Actually, the parties really aren't that exciting. I only have them because I'm supposed to. I'd really like you to be there to keep me company. I feel so out of place at them, but I think I'd feel more comfortable if you were there."

"Maybe I'll stay, then. But just one more night," Lucy said with a smile.

The next morning, the maid took Lucy to a great room full of ball gowns. They were made of the finest fabrics and came in a variety of different colors. It was difficult to choose, but the maid helped her find one that suited Lucy nicely. It was a bright blue silk dress with a pale blue sash around the waist. When Lucy went to show Damien her dress, he went into the royal jewel room and found her a beautiful pair of sapphire earrings and a matching necklace.

"A thank-you gift for agreeing to stay," he told her.

"Oh no, I couldn't..." she said.

"No, I insist. They just gather dust here. I'd rather someone beautiful be wearing them."

Lucy felt her face grow warm with a blush. "Thank you. But tomorrow morning I must leave to find my home."

"If you insist," Damien said sadly. "At least I'll see you tonight."

That evening, the guests for the ball began to arrive in great carriages driven by the most beautiful white animals Lucy had ever seen: white horses and white giraffes and white elephants, just to name a few. The guests were even more beautiful, all dressed their best in gowns as fine as Lucy's. But even though Lucy was dressed in the same glamour as everyone else, she felt very out of place at the ball. She longed to find her way home.

She quickly found Damien. "I'm sorry, I can't stay. I don't belong here."

"No, please. Don't leave now," Damien pleaded, and took her hands in his. "I don't feel like I belong here either—except when I'm with you."

"But...this is your castle. Your home," Lucy told him.

Damien looked around—at the fancy guests and crystal chandeliers. He shrugged. "I don't feel very at home here."

"I'm sorry," she said. "But neither do I. I have to go. Now."

She pushed past all the guests and out the doors, into the night. She ran to the cornfield and into the maze, the cornstalks standing tall just above her head. She kept running and running. Her beautiful dress kept catching on the cornstalks and ripping. It was a dark, moonless night, but she kept running. She could hear the sound of a train whistle, and she ran toward it. The cornstalks began to grow taller and taller, blocking out even the feeble light from the stars. The train whistle was getting louder, and then she could see the paved path—the one she had stood on that sunny day, where the rollerbladers and bicyclists zoomed by. That seemed like ages ago. She shoved the cornstalks aside and stepped out onto the path, just as the train thundered by.

"I'm home," she whispered to herself. But it still didn't feel quite right.

A group of teenagers walked by and whistled at her. "Nice dress. Where ya' going? The prom?"

Lucy shook her head and collapsed in exhaustion. The teenagers snickered and kept walking. This was not her home. Yes, it was where she started, but it wasn't her home. She fiddled with her sapphire necklace and looked toward the cornfield. The wind rustled the stalks, and the voice called her name: "Lucy..."

She stood up and stepped back into the cornfield maze. She had to find her home.

"Lucy..." she heard someone calling. She looked up, but it wasn't the fork–tailed white bird, or the emerald green bird. There was no one to be seen. The cornstalks didn't grow. Lucy wandered until she came out of the maze and onto a sandy beach.

A tiny little cottage stood there.

"Lucy..." the voice called again, but she couldn't tell from which direction it came. She walked on, and felt the sand beneath her feet. The waves sang music, crashing against the shore.

"Lucy! I've found you," came the voice. It was Damien.

"What...What are you doing here?" she asked.

Damien looked around. "Is this your home?" he asked.

"No. I found my home, but it wasn't really..."

"It's beautiful here," Damien said.

Lucy looked around. She took a deep breath. She looked at the sparkling water, and then back to Damien: "Yes. I think this is my home."

Damien held Lucy's hand. She squeezed his hand and smiled.

"I think this is my home, too," Damien said.

I slip and fall into the water. Again. The salt water fills my nose, makes its way down my throat. I get back on my feet, cough up the water. I slick back the curtain of black hair that has fallen over my eyes.

I can hear my classmates around me laugh and joke, splashing in the water, playing childish games. None of them are taking it seriously. I stare out at the horizon, trying to steady my aching legs, bracing myself against the ebb and flow of the ocean's waves. I wish I could join in the games with some of the other boys, but they'll just laugh at me. They know I can't swim.

I don't want to slip into the water again, but my legs have always been unsteady, weak—my left leg considerably shorter than my right leg, and the muscles in my arms and legs don't grow strong like other children. The elders say it is a disease that runs in my family, that my grandfather was the same as me. The elders say my grandfather could never swim.

The waves are strong and continue to knock me off balance. The stones beneath my feet are slippery. I envy the other students, the ones who can swim out into the deeps, treading water, strong legs keeping them afloat. We're out here today to practice our swimming, but I'm not allowed out of the shallows. I've never been able to swim, to keep my head above water.

"There!" a classmate says, pointing out into the ocean. "I see one!"

The sea beast swims out in the deeps, farther than any of my classmates have ever dared to swim. The sun reflects on its shining green scales, making them sparkle. The beast's long neck surfaces, its head large and slender. It dives back into the water, its serpentine-like body following it back into the ocean. It continues this pattern, playing in the waves. Another appears alongside it, and another. Soon there is a group of five, swimming in and out of the water, like my grandmother pulling a needle and thread.

"Soon it'll be your chance," our teacher tells us. "One day, not far from now, we will find out who among you will be a Sea Rider, like your most noble ancestors."

I watch the sea beasts swim out in the ocean, elegant and powerful. They've been a part of our people's history for centuries. It is a great honor to be a Sea Rider, to become a partner with one of the beasts, and join the ranks of the other great and powerful Sea Riders who guard our island from intruders—pillaging pirates, and other monsters of the deep. Only after you fail at becoming a Sea Rider does anyone ever consider another livelihood.

Months pass, and my class has come of age. We will be tested. We will find out who among us will make a connection with one of the great sea beasts and become Sea Riders.

"Not you, Hunakai," my teacher says, as I kick off my sandals and begin to wade into the ocean. I stop, feeling the cool waves lap at my ankles.

I watch my classmates run into the water, splashing each other, diving headfirst into the waves and kicking their powerful legs, swimming away from me. I reluctantly nod to my teacher. I walk back to the shore and take a seat on the sandy beach.

"We always need good, smart workers to do shore tasks," my teacher says, speaking of the people who never become Sea Riders. "You are a very bright boy. You will be sure to find something you are useful at."

I watch as my classmates swim out into the ocean, to where the unclaimed sea beasts play. If they approach one and the animal accepts them, they will be partners for life—they will be Sea Riders. I see my classmate Aluna is the first to attempt to form a partnership with one of the giant creatures. She is the tallest in our class, and strong. She is the best swimmer, and is unafraid to swim out farther and farther, until she reaches a pair of green sea beasts. She approaches the first one, and steadies herself, treading water. She reaches out a hand, but the sea beast turns away and splashes her as it dives under the waves. She coughs up some water, and then waits. The other sea beast has stayed above water, watching her. She doesn't put out her hand this time, but the sea beast comes closer. When it is close enough to touch, she runs her hand along one of its large, green scales. The sea beast looks at her with its huge, black eyes. Aluna looks back to our teacher, who gives her a nod.

Aluna places both hands on the sea beast, just below its neck, and pulls herself up onto its back. The sea beast stays steady in the water for her. My classmates erupt into cheers. Aluna will be the island's newest Sea Rider.

I sit on the beach. It's night, and no one else is out this late. Out of my class, four were chosen to be Sea Riders. I am now learning how to run the farm with my uncle. There's a lot to learn about crops and weather patterns. I can't do much of the physical labor, but my uncle says he needs someone with a good head on his shoulders to keep things running smoothly. I find it interesting, and I enjoy my uncle's company, but all I ever dream about is the ocean. I wake up in the night and can't go back to sleep. I only feel right when I sit on the beach, my feet submerged in the salty water. I yearn to go deeper into the waves, but I know it's dangerous—I can't swim, and not even the strong swimmers are supposed to swim at night, alone.

Tonight I can see a couple of sea beasts out on the horizon, dipping in and out of the water, the faint moonlight making their scales softly sparkle. I think about Aluna, and how she has been training with the Sea Riders—every day she goes farther and farther out into the ocean with her sea beast. I throw a rock into the water. I feel angry and jealous. I wasn't even given a chance. They're supposed to let everyone try, but I wasn't even allowed to try. I couldn't. There was no way for me to swim out that far into the ocean. I would help on the farm for the rest of my life. I would be a land worker. I would never leave the island.

Something catches my eye. Another sea beast has appeared, but it's much closer than the others. I try to keep my eyes fixed on it. It continues to dive under the waves, disappears, and then comes back up again—closer and closer. It's the closest I've ever seen a sea beast come to shore, and it continues on its course.

It stops. It's only a few meters from the shoreline. It can't come any closer. It's too big, and the water too shallow. It's staring at me, the moon reflecting in its huge, black eyes. It looks like its scales are a very dark green, almost black, but it's hard to tell in the dim moonlight. I stand and begin to enter the ocean, my legs as unsteady as always. The water where the sea beast is would be just under my chin. I've never been out that far. If I slip, I might not be able to get my head above the surface again. But the sea beast hasn't taken its eyes off of me. I continue my slow progress toward it.

I feel a sudden tug on my ankle, on my bad leg. I've stumbled into a clump of seaweed, the tendrils snaking around my ankle. I struggle to free myself, but I lose my balance and fall. My head plunges under the water and I accidentally breathe in the salt water. I sit up, and my head is out of water again. I cough and gasp for breath. The sea beast is still watching me, patiently. I get back on my feet. I'm moving even slower than before, the water getting deeper, the waves stronger. The water is at my neck now. I can almost reach out and touch one of creature's dark green scales.

I slip again. This time the water is too deep and I plunge under the waves. My legs kick uselessly. I flail my arms around and I feel my hands come in contact with the sea beast's smooth scales. I pull myself onto it and I feel the giant animal moving, swimming, bringing me up to the surface.

I'm on its back. I cough and gasp again, and readjust myself so I don't slip off. It turns its head to look back at me, and blinks slowly. I wrap my arms around its neck, and it begins to swim into the ocean, farther and farther out.

The sea beast has chosen me. I will be a Sea Rider.

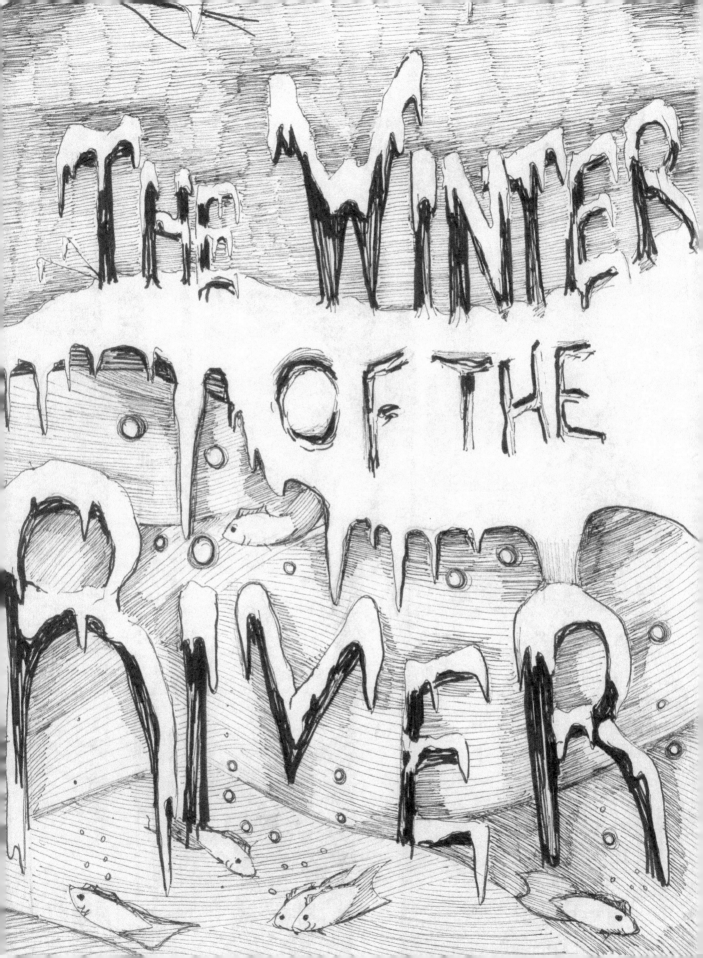

Will went running over to Mary's house, ice skates swinging over his shoulder. He pounded on the front door. Mary answered the door with a smile, her long golden hair draping down her back in a pair of messy braids.

"What is it, Will?" she asked.

Will looked to the sky, a wry smile on his face, as snowflakes drifted down around him. "It's been snowing and cold for a week now, Mary. I think the river will be frozen."

"I'll get my skates."

The two children headed down their street to the river that ran through the little meadow, ice skates over their shoulders.

"What happened? There..." Will asked Mary, as he brushed a piece of stray hair away to reveal a bruise on her cheek.

"Oh, I fell," she said.

Will laughed. "For someone who skates as good as you do, you're an awful klutz off the ice."

"Yeah..." Mary said, and laughed lightly.

A small forest of trees surrounded the narrow river. They pushed through them, and then slid down the snowy bank to the ice.

"You test it," Mary said, pointing to the river.

"But of course," Will said. He bowed to her, and then gingerly stepped out onto the snow-covered river. "Feels frozen," he said, and did a few little jumps and stomps. The ice held.

Mary grinned and began removing her boots to trade them for skates. Will sat down beside her and began to do the same. As soon as Mary was done, she glided onto the ice.

"Beat you," she said. She spun around as Will finished tying his skates. He got to his feet, gliding out to join her.

"Think you're so fast—race you to that log," Will said, and before he could say, "Go!" Mary was off.

Will whipped by her, and she ended up reaching the log a few seconds behind him.

"Race you back to our boots?" Will said, but Mary was staring off into the distance.

"What is it?" Will asked.

"Where does the river go?" she asked him.

Will looked down the river. They could see where it made a bend in its path, but not any farther. The trees arched overhead, snow gently sprinkling down through their branches.

"I don't know where the river goes," Will said.

"Well, we could find out, couldn't we?"

"I don't know, Mary. I told my mom we'd just be on the river..."

"We will be on the river."

"I mean, the river here, by the meadow."

Mary frowned. "But I want to know." She started skating away.

"Mary! No!" Will said, and grabbed at her coat sleeve.

"Come on, Will. Where's your sense of adventure?"

Will looked down at his hockey skates. "Mary, I think we should just stay here. Why can't we just skate like we usually do?"

"I'm tired of skating like we usually do," Mary told him stubbornly.

"But it's our first skate of the season!" Will protested.

"I'm going to find out where the river goes. Come or stay, it's up to you," Mary said, and skated off, leaving Will behind.

Will's thoughts raced. Should he go with her to make sure the ice was safe? Follow her and try to convince her to come back? Or stay where he had told his mother he would be? But his mother would probably yell at him for letting Mary go off on her own.

"Mary! Mary, wait!" Will called, and skated after her.

Mary did a twirl on the ice and faced her friend. "I knew you'd come," she said with a grin and started off again.

The trees began to get closer together, forming an archway over their heads, and blocking out the light from above. It grew dark.

"Mary, maybe we've gone far enough. Maybe we should go back," Will said. He was getting tired and falling farther and farther behind her.

"Just a little bit more!" Mary called.

And then there was a CRACK!

Mary screamed and disappeared under the ice.

"Mary!" Will cried. He skated to the edge of the hole and slid to his knees, peering into the water. "Mary!" He couldn't see her anywhere.

Suddenly an ice-white hand reached out from the depths, grabbed Will by his scarf and pulled him under before he even had a chance to scream.

Will found himself floating—floating down through an astonishingly deep depth of water, yet he was comfortably warm and able to breathe. It was much brighter beneath the ice. He looked below him, and saw Mary floating down too, her eyes shut and body limp. Sparkling white fish swam around him, making soft cooing noises. Will couldn't spot who had pulled him under.

"Mary!" he called. The word swam out of his mouth and down to his friend and spiraled along her body, yet her eyes remained closed. The word continued falling, to the river floor. Strange white trees grew down there, with white bark and sparkly snowballs hanging from their delicate branches, tiny snowflakes falling from each.

Mary's body gracefully reached the river floor, and she lay there, in the white snow. Will gently landed beside her, but just as he was about to reach over to her, someone smacked him out of the way. Will went rolling head-over-heels into a tree trunk. When his head cleared, he saw a skinny boy clad in a white three-piece suit sitting next to Mary, his head inclined over hers.

"What are you doing?" Will called to him, as he jumped to his feet. The new boy's head snapped up and tilted to the side, catlike. In his pale white face were startlingly large blue eyes that bore uncomfortably into Will's.

"I'm going to help her," the boy told him.

"Is she going to be okay?" Will asked. "Where are we?"

"Ssshhhh," the boy said to Will, and then turned back to Mary. He leaned down his head until his lips almost met hers—but Will pushed him away.

"Stop it!" Will said.

The boy snarled at him. "Do you want her to die?" he asked.

"No, of course not!" Will said.

"Then let me help her."

Will watched warily as the skinny boy leaned over Mary once more, and laid a kiss on her lips. Mary blinked and opened her eyes.

"Will?" she said.

"I'm here," Will told her, and helped her sit up.

"Where am I? Who are you?" she asked the boy.

"My name's Jack, and you are in Unwinderly," he said. He sprang to his feet to bow. "And you, my dear, shall be my queen," Jack said, and offered his hand for her to take. But she declined.

Mary turned to Will. "Am I dreaming?"

Will didn't answer her. Instead he turned to Jack: "What do you mean she shall be your queen?"

Jack folded his skinny arms and tapped his foot, giving a reproachful look to Will.

"If a mortal girl falls through my ice, I get to make her my queen. And you, boy, shall be my servant."

"What if we don't want to stay here?" Will asked.

"You don't have a choice," Jack told him, and tilted his head upwards. Above them was a sky of thick, gray ice.

"We can live down here?" Mary asked.

"Yes! Of course you may live here, my queen!" Jack said.

"Mary, we have to go home. Our parents will worry," Will said.

Mary ignored Will and stood. She took a step toward Jack, who smiled and made a loud whistle. A sleigh pulled by three large, silvery-white fish arrived. Jack offered his hand to Mary, and this time she accepted. Jack helped her into the sleigh, and then got in beside her. He took the reins in his hands and ordered the fish to swim. Will skated after them, desperate to keep Mary in sight.

Jack drove the sleigh to a brilliant cathedral made of ice and snow. Will watched in despair as Mary accepted her new role as the Queen of Unwinderly, and married Jack. They had a great wedding party that all the fish attended, and Mary wore a magnificent gown of white and silver.

Will skated off and lived amongst a school of silver-blue fish, but was forced to do chores for King Jack. Mary was always dressed in beautiful gowns, and skated along with Jack, laughing and playing games. Over time, she nearly forgot about poor Will, until one night when he snuck into her room through the window while Jack was out and about doing King-Jack-things.

"Mary, I've got an idea to escape," he told her. "Come with me."

"Will?" she asked, for she hadn't seen him in so long. "I've missed you, Will!"

"Then come with me now, and we can leave," he told her eagerly.

"Leave? But I like it here. No one hurts me here."

"What do you mean? Mary, this isn't your home. Come home with me. Now!"

Mary hung her head, blond strands covering her face. "Will, you may leave if you like, and I won't tell Jack. But please, let me stay here."

"But, Mary..."

"Please, Will," she said, and then they heard footsteps coming to the door. "It's Jack. You best be off. Goodbye, Will. I'll miss you always."

"And I you," Will said, and quickly kissed her forehead before skating away.

Will had seen a crack in the ice that day. He took the axe he used to cut firewood for Jack, and began to swim to the frozen surface while the kingdom slept. He swung the axe at the ice and broke his way through. As soon as he did, icy cold water filled his lungs. He pushed himself to the surface, gasping for air and sopping wet. All the way home he shivered in the cold, as warm tears streamed down his face.

I know she'll change her mind and come back someday, Will thought to himself. And I'll be there, waiting.

Every day, Will would visit the little river. Spring came, yet the river stayed frozen, and snow hung from the branches of the trees. Summer came too, and every day Will would walk through a meadow of wild flowers to the winter of the river, expecting to find Mary there, but all he found was the quiet, frozen river.

Years passed, and every day of every year, Will would visit the river. He refused to give up, even though he was growing old. He still dreamed of her often, skating along the river with her braids trailing behind. If it wasn't for the dreams, Will feared he'd forget what she looked like, her hair so bright and golden.

One day in mid-August, when all the birds were singing, Will made his way down to the river. The trees around the river had no leaves, and snow gently fell to the ground among them.

"Mary..." Will called softly, as he always did, but nothing happened. He was leaving when he heard a sharp CRACK! He quickly turned.

The ice had split open, and from it rose a beautiful young girl clad in a magnificent white and silver dress. He would barely have been able to see her against the winter scene, had it not been for her golden hair.

"Will?" she asked softly.

"Yes," Will said, taking a step forward. "Mary?"

The girl nodded, and Will rushed forward and embraced her, then released her and looked upon her face. She appeared as young as the day he had last skated with her.

"You haven't aged," he said, astounded.

"Below the ice, I am immortal," she explained.

"And have you come up now, to come away with me? To leave horrid Unwinderly?" he asked.

"Unwinderly is not a horrid place," she told him. "I've come to talk to you."

Will was crestfallen she still didn't want to leave. "And what do
you have to say?"

"Will..." she said calmly. "You have to let me go."

"Let you go?"

"Yes, stop holding on to me, Will. Stop coming back to the river every day, looking for me. You have to let your love for me go."

"But Mary, that's impossible," Will said. "I've loved you forever."

"You have to move on. We live in different worlds now. We have now for years. Decades," Mary said.

"But we don't have to. You can come back."

Mary shook her head. "I can't come back now. I've been immortal for too long. The strain of returning to this world permanently would kill me."

"Please, Mary, don't make me do this," Will pleaded.

"But you must, for the sake of the river. It's winter all year long because you won't let me go. Set me free, Will, let the river return to its natural course."

"I don't want to," Will said.

"Sometimes you must do things you don't want to do," she told him gently.

They were silent for a moment. Will nodded and hugged her one last time. "If it's best for you..."

"It is," she assured him.

"Then...Then I let you go," he told her. Before the words had even left his lips, Mary had vanished. The ice began to melt. Will quickly ran to the bank so he wouldn't fall into the river. The snow melted off the trees and buds began to grow, bright and green. The grass began to sprout. All around him summer began to bloom, and the river began to flow. Will looked down the river, to where it was flowing around the corner, and wondered where it led to. He began walking along the bank, to find out.

1. Josh remembered the tree as a little sapling in his parents' backyard. It slowly grew toward the sky. By the time Josh was seven, he could climb among its branches. He even fell once and broke his arm. Then, when he was twelve, he woke up one day and looked out in his backyard, and the tree was gone.

2. Rodney was a fisherman's son, off the coast of Newfoundland. He was on his father's boat when he saw the tree, roots and all, floating in the ocean. He told his mom about the tree over dinner that night. She thought it sounded like an odd thing to see and passed the peas.

3. Maddy's kite blew into the tree. The tree shook its branches and let the kite glide back to her waiting, outstretched hands. Then it left the park, to continue on its way. "Thank you!" Maddy had called after it.

4. All Pierre remembered was waking up to see a full-sized tree in the center of his front lawn one morning, where no tree had been before. He rushed off to the bus stop, so he wouldn't be late for school (again). When he got home later that day, the tree was gone.

5. A squirrel once tried to make a nest in the tree. She didn't like the constant change of scenery and decided to raise her young elsewhere.

6. Sophia was in the forest with her black lab, Marty, taking an autumn stroll. She saw the tree move among the tall oaks. Marty barked and tried to chase it, but Sophia called him back. When she got home she told herself she must have just been seeing things.

7. Neal followed the tree. He was wandering late at night, as he often did (much to his mother's worry). Fluffy snowflakes gently began to fall, occasionally illuminated by the streetlights. Neal saw the tree stroll down an alley and he knew he had to follow. He slowed down as he got closer, staying a bit behind the tree.

The city was quiet, fast asleep. Not a single car in the street. Buses had stopped running hours ago. It was the time of night that Neal loved best.

The tree, roots crunching in the thick layer of snow that had already covered the ground, made its way down the road. Its winter branches were bare of leaves, but now heavy in white snowflakes.

Neal followed closer as they entered the streets of suburbia, full of large Victorian houses with their pointed turrets, decorative trim, and grand porches. The tree moved steadily and swiftly. With purpose. Neal was practically jogging to keep up with the tree, and then BAM, his sneakered foot slid on a sheet of dark ice and he went crashing to the ground.

"Ouch," Neal mumbled, as he lay on the ice.

Neal sat up, feeling pain throb through his tailbone. He heard the snow crunching and looked up to see the tree looming above him. The tree lowered a branch down to Neal. Neal, amazed, took hold and the tree helped him to his feet.

The tree didn't have eyes, but Neal felt its gaze upon him.

"Why?" Neal asked.

"Sometimes," the tree said softly, though where its voice came from he did not know, "it's good to do something no one ever believed you could do."

"Huh," Neal said, and the tree continued on its way.

Author

Elizabeth J.M. Walker has always loved reading and writing. She lives in Windsor, Ontario with her husband and their dog and two cats. Elizabeth is the author of the books **She Dreamed of Dragons, This Night Sucks, Slip Jig Summer**, and **The Boy Who Owned the Forest**.

Illustrator

Nicholas Beckett has been drawing since he can remember. For a while now he has been making zines of his and other people's stories as a way of getting his work out into the world. Most recently, after completing 1000 protesting figures, he has taken them on the road as part of the Redfern Fringe Biennale, a solo international art festival. He lives in Sydney Australia.

Previously published in:

The Boy Who Owned the Forest – published in 398, Issue 3, 2003; and 398, Issue 10, 2008; and The Boy Who Owned the Forest (with illustrations by Nicholas Beckett), 2012.

The Piano that Swam – published in 398, Issue 6, 2004; and 398, Issue 10, 2008.

Cornelia and Timothy and the Wonderful World of Zines – published in 398, Issue 8, 2006; and 398, Issue 10, 2008; and Stinkwaves Magazine, Volume 4, Issue 1, 2016.

The Maze – published in 398, Issue 3, 2003; and 398, Issue 10, 2008; and The Maze (with illustrations by Nicholas Beckett), 2013.

The Sea Rider – published in Realms YA Fantasy Literary Magazine, Issue 1, 2015.

The Winter of the River – published in 398, Issue 5, 2004; and 398, Issue 10, 2008; and Stinkwaves Magazine, Volume 5, Issue 1, 2017.

The Tree – published in 398, Issue 10, 2008.

Thank you for purchasing and reading *The Boy Who Owned the Forest*. Handersen Publishing is an independent publishing house that specializes in creating quality young adult, middle grade, and picture books. We hope you enjoyed this book and will consider leaving a review on Amazon or Goodreads. A small review can make a big difference. Thank you.

CPSIA information can be obtained
at www.ICGtesting.com
Printed in the USA
LVHW102031030419
612868LV00009B/31/P

9 781947 854376

.